Once Upon A Wave
A Surf Story

Written by
Roberto Diaz

Paintings by
Howard Kirk

Published by

Olas
Small Books for
Big Imaginations

www.olasbooks.com
(866) 238-7759

Copyright ©2007 by Olas Enterprises, Inc., A California Corporation
PO Box 919 Dana Point, CA 92629

ISBN 0-9764788-8-9

Library of Congress Control Number: 2006936252

Acknowledgments

To my beautiful, muse Marla. Thank you for all the love that you have poured into Olas, for being my best friend and inspiration. I love you!

To my first-born, Garrett, thank you for coming into my life. I am so happy to be in this journey with you!

A special thanks to Karen Wilson for her mentoring, editing and above all, her friendship. You gave me strength when I needed it most!

Howard, your patience, commitment and trust was essential in getting this project off the ground. Thank you from the bottom of my heart!

I would also like to thank Jonathan at Free Wheel Chair Mission, a wonderful non-profit organization, Dava Romaniello for her creative graphic designs, Rick and Debbie of Comline Marketing for spreading the word about our books. Also to Rob Machado and his agent Justine Chiara, Robert and Sam August, Richard Chew and Janine Robinson thank you for your generosity with your time.

Many MAHALOS to Dean and Ingrid of Venus Surf Adventures for all DA KOKUA!

Thank you Laguna Beach Surf Mamas for always giving us your support. Marla and I love you all!

To my nephews and nieces: JR, JP, Abby and Raquel Anne; Crystal, Raquel Alexis and Steven Michael; Noah and Jalen. Thank you for helping me stay young at heart.

Last, but not least, I am thankful to the CREATOR for all the people, love, prosperity, health and waves in my life!

Once upon a wave,

there surfed a young *grom* named Moe.

Grom: *Derives from grommet, a protective swimming plug, and is used to describe any young surfer, skater or snowboarder.*

Moe loved to surf.

He began riding waves on his belly while he was still learning to talk.

He lived with his family close to the beach, which made it easy for him to surf often.

By the time Moe was 12, he was one of the best surfers around.

But one day, Moe found himself in trouble. He was paddling hard, but could not move from the same spot. As he tried to get to the beach, the ocean seemed to pull him into its depths. No one else was out in the water near him and the sky was covered with dark clouds.

The ocean felt strange, Moe thought to himself. It did not want to let him go.

Moe whined to himself, *"Dude, I totally feel like a hamster in a hamster wheel. I am paddling like a maniac! "*

Moe was afraid because he had never paddled out alone. He knew that he was supposed to surf with someone else and stay close to the lifeguard tower. But today, instead of waiting for his Uncle Kawika to pick him up, Moe decided to go to the beach by himself for the first time. He had surfed his home break a hundred times. So Moe felt it would be safe to surf alone.

The ocean was calm at first. Moe just wanted to catch a few waves. Catching waves was more fun than the coolest rollercoaster ride, more thrilling than any goal he had ever scored on a soccer field, more satisfying than the best candy he had ever eaten. Riding waves made everything better. Surfing was the thing he loved to do most in the whole wide world. But now, in the ocean, all alone, Moe was afraid.

As far back as Moe could remember he had always heard surf stories. From his dad and his mom, to his uncles and aunties, to the lifeguard at his home break, friends and family had always told him stories about staying safe in the ocean.

Moe thought he knew everything there was to know about surfing!

Moe thought that their surf stories were silly.

"I am a great surfer!" Moe would say to his friends. Moe thought since he was a better surfer than most of his friends, he knew how to take care of himself in the ocean without anyone's help.

Always surf in places appropriate to your surfing abilities. If you are just learning how to surf, go to a gentler breaking wave that is not so steep or filled with surfers that have loads of experience.

Years ago, his Auntie Tia told Moe,

"Always watch the surf before you go out. Sometimes, there are lulls in between the sets. A lull is a period in between the sets where waves are not rolling in. You may think that there are not any waves or that the surf is very small, but it is just that you are watching it while the lull is happening. So, Sweetie, always watch the ocean before you jump in the waves."

Tia had told Moe that once, when she was first learning to surf, she decided to catch a few waves after work. In a hurry, because soon it would be dark, she jumped right in the water without checking the surf first. By the time she got to the lineup, she realized that it was way bigger than she thought it was. In fact, she had never seen a wave break so far out. Auntie Tia was right on the impact zone about to get buried by the force of rolling white water from a big wave that had just closed out in front of her.

The Line-up: The place outside of the breaking wave where wave riders wait for the coming waves.

The Impact Zone: Place on the water's surface where the falling lip of the wave hits the water.
Waves break here most frequently and can be the most challenging place in the ocean.

Listen to Moe's Auntie and always look at the ocean's conditions before you jump in the water. The bigger the surf,
the more time you should spend watching the surf. Ten minutes is a good guideline.

She was so frightened! She paddled hard with all her might away from shore towards open ocean. She built enough speed to duck dive the closed out set.   Her arms were hurting from paddling so hard, but she kept paddling anyway. As she looked towards the horizon, the only thing she could see was a giant wall of water coming straight for her.

Now, she began to paddle even harder than before, harder than she had ever paddled in her entire life.   The set wave began to rise and rise, and her board rose with the wave. She started to fear that she and her board would be tossed backwards as the lip began to pitch.

Close Out: *When the wave breaks straight down without any definite direction. It is the direct opposite of a peaking wave and there is really no place for a surfer to ride but straight to the beach.*

Do you know what duck diving is?

All of a sudden, she broke through the top, and felt her board dropping down the back of the huge, monster wave. Tia had gone past the impact zone and had finally made it to the outside.

Her relief lasted only a minute, when she noticed that there were not many people in the water. She was far out and the waves were closing out on the shore. No one was around her.

Tia was terrified of the shore break! The waves were big and making a loud sound when they pounded hard on the sand. Suddenly, an old Hawaiian surfer paddled over. He noticed how afraid Tia looked. The old Hawaiian surfer rode a big wooden board like the ones the ancient surfers use to ride. He had a big hard belly and a round face with a stringy wet beard. When he spoke, his voice immediately made her feel calm.

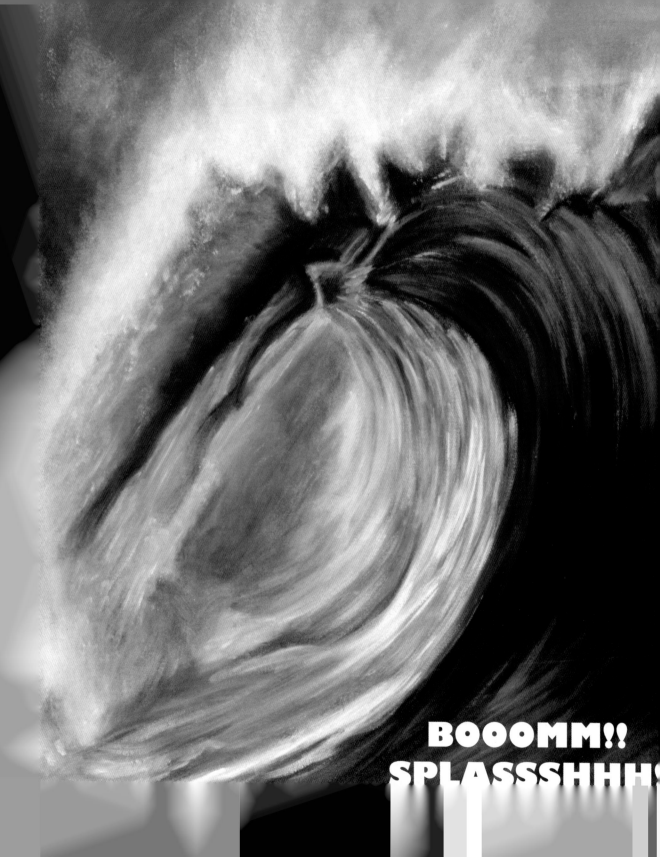

BOOOMM!!
SPLASSSHHH!

The old Hawaiian said with a thick islander accent, *"Aloha, sistah. Da nalu stay big, but no sked! I goin help you back to da beach safe!"* He explained to Tia that if she waited patiently for the lull to come, she could paddle herself in while there weren't any waves coming.

They both sat out there for a while and waited as the sets thundered in. Then as the Hawaiian scanned the horizon, he told Tia, *"Ok, we get one lull! Go in, paddle hard for da beach!"*

Tia paddled fast, looking back once in a while over her shoulder to see if a set wave was going to crash on her head. Yet, the only waves that came fizzled onto the beach with a gentle splash. The old Hawaiian's wisdom had helped Tia make it to shore safe and sound.

Auntie Tia told Moe that this man had helped her by watching the sets and timing how often the *nalus* were coming in. From that day on, she made a habit of watching the surf before going out, like a ritual.

Auntie still likes to keep track of how big the *nalus* are, how many *nalus* per set, and how long the lulls are in between.

Surfing has been practiced in Hawaii for hundreds of years, tracing its roots back to Polynesian ancestors who were gifted watermen.

Nalu: Means wave in the ancient Hawaiian tongue.

*Did you know that the word for **nalu** in Spanish is **olas**?*

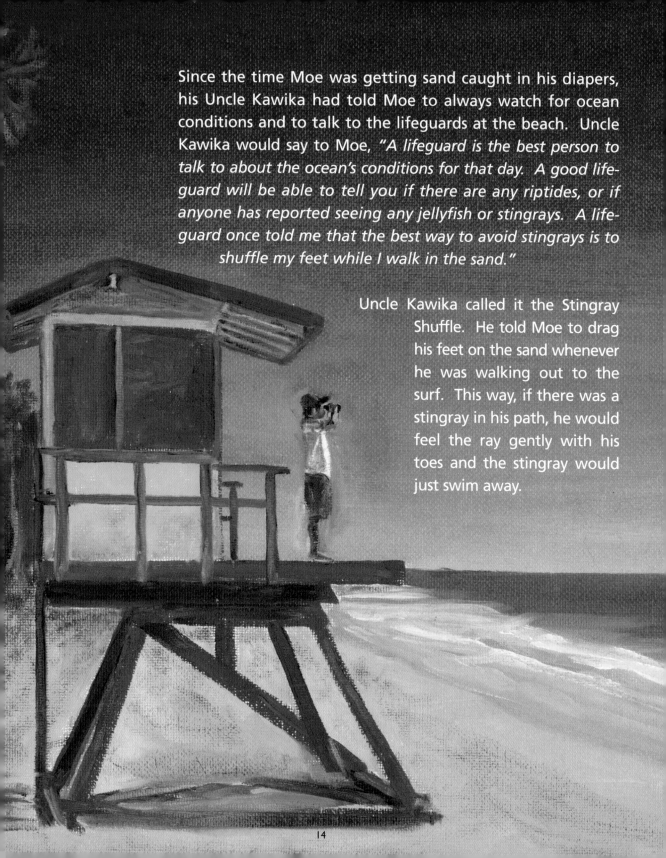

Since the time Moe was getting sand caught in his diapers, his Uncle Kawika had told Moe to always watch for ocean conditions and to talk to the lifeguards at the beach. Uncle Kawika would say to Moe, *"A lifeguard is the best person to talk to about the ocean's conditions for that day. A good lifeguard will be able to tell you if there are any riptides, or if anyone has reported seeing any jellyfish or stingrays. A lifeguard once told me that the best way to avoid stingrays is to shuffle my feet while I walk in the sand."*

Uncle Kawika called it the Stingray Shuffle. He told Moe to drag his feet on the sand whenever he was walking out to the surf. This way, if there was a stingray in his path, he would feel the ray gently with his toes and the stingray would just swim away.

Moe was usually very careful whenever he went surfing. He always checked the flags to see what the conditions were like.

The flag Moe liked the least was yellow with a black ball in the middle.

Do you know what this flag means?

It means **no surfing!**

Checking the flags that are posted by lifeguards is a quick way of learning the conditions for surfing. Flags are sort of like traffic light

GREEN means safe to GO   YELLOW means be CAREFUL   RED means DANGEROUS

Today, Moe did not see any flags and he later realized it was because all the lifeguards had gone home for the day.

Moe thought to himself, *"Man, that was not the smartest move! This is more like something my little brother Jalen would do."*

Jalen was just learning how to surf. He was a total beginner and would constantly get in trouble for not listening to those around him who had more experience. Almost every weekend, Jalen asked Moe to take him to the beach. When they did go together, they always went with a grown-up.

Moe's older cousin Noah would sometimes surf with both Jalen and Moe. Cousin Noah was one of the best surfers around. Even better than Moe. Cousin Noah would take the gnarliest drops, catch the sickest tube rides and launch the biggest airs Jalen and Moe had ever seen.

Air: Any maneuver that has the surfer and board in the air above the wave.

Tube Ride: Also referred to as getting barreled, shacked, shaded, in the green room. It is when the surfer sits inside the breaking wave as the upper lip of the wave breaks above the surfer's head. Many surfers feel this is the most classy and exciting maneuver in surfing.

When the three of them went surfing, Moe always reminded Jalen to stay close to shore. Once, when Jalen was first learning to surf, his leash broke. A set of waves washed up Jalen's surfboard all the way to the beach and he was out past the impact zone. It was the first time Jalen had been that far out in the ocean without a board. Suddenly, he realized how much he depended on the board for help. Without a board, he had to constantly swim to stay above water.

Leashes break for a variety of reasons: sometimes they break because the leash gets cut by the sharp edge of the fin; sometimes, they break because they are old and worn out; sometimes, they just seem to snap for no apparent reason.

Smart idea: Rinse your leash after every session to remove corrosive salt water and replace it every year with a new leash.

Lifeguards advise young and new surfers alike to surf close to shore. In case their board is lost, they can easily swim to safety. Even experienced surfers need to remember that if their energy level is low, they are putting themselves at great risk by surfing far from shore.

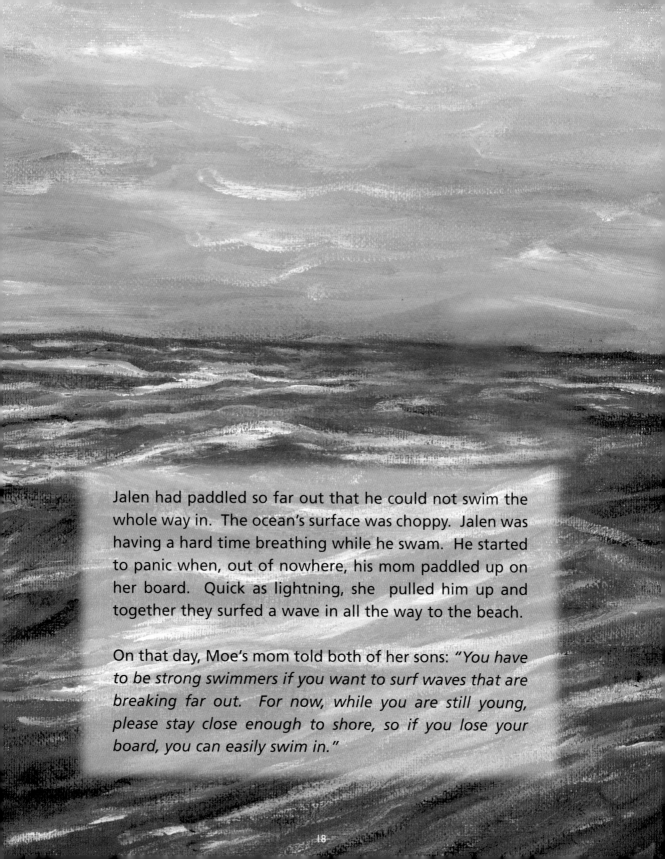

Jalen had paddled so far out that he could not swim the whole way in. The ocean's surface was choppy. Jalen was having a hard time breathing while he swam. He started to panic when, out of nowhere, his mom paddled up on her board. Quick as lightning, she pulled him up and together they surfed a wave in all the way to the beach.

On that day, Moe's mom told both of her sons: *"You have to be strong swimmers if you want to surf waves that are breaking far out. For now, while you are still young, please stay close enough to shore, so if you lose your board, you can easily swim in."*

Moe remembered his mom's words of wisdom. But, today, the beach was so close, and yet it felt very far away. The harder Moe paddled to make it to shore, the more tired he grew. With all his effort, he was still not getting closer to the beach.

It was hard for Moe to imagine how he found himself in trouble in the ocean. Moe was always so careful.

Whenever Moe would jump off his board at the end of a ride, Moe always protected his head. If he was going over the falls, he would curl up like a ball or try to land on his rear end, the softest spot to land on. Whenever Moe surfed over coral, he would always make sure to plane out when falling, so that he would not sink deep and hit the coral reef. By spreading his arms and legs when falling in the water, Moe stayed close to the surface. Moe had heard plenty of stories of surfers who would get injured because they did not protect themselves when they fell off their boards.

Over The Falls: Describes going over the lip of a barreling wave.

Now, not only was Moe scared, but he felt stupid for making such a silly mistake. Moe knew better. He kept asking himself, *"How did I get myself in trouble?"* The waves were the biggest he had ever seen and night was starting to fall.

Moe was upset with himself for making a mistake, but being upset was making things worse. Moe remembered a story he had heard from his father. His dad had gone out on a really big day. Gale winds swirled water with immense force. Massive swells had formed from a great storm in the rough seas of the Southern Hemisphere. It was the Storm of the Century!

It is important in emergency situations to focus on the solution.

As Moe's dad sat on the outside waiting for a wave, he realized that he was moving quite fast from his line-up spot on land. Normally, he would keep an eye out on a fixed land object so that he could tell exactly where he was catching the waves. Not only was it the best way to stay on the peak, but this line-up spot would let him know how fast the current was moving. Moe's dad would usually choose a tall palm tree or a big house on the beach. That day he had chosen an old lighthouse that sat empty on this cove.

Looking at the lighthouse from his position in the water, Moe's dad realized that he was drifting. The water surrounding him was moving quite fast in the direction opposite to where he wanted to go.

The Peak: Refers to the highest point of a wave. It is the point that will begin to curl or break first. Staying on the peak helps a surfer catch waves with the least amount of paddling.

A Line-up Spot: Place in the water where it is easiest to catch waves. It is determined by using fixed land spots which helps surfers determine their current position in the water.

Moe remembered his dad telling him, *"I had never before been caught in such a strong rip current!"*

"Oh, man!! That's it! I am caught in a rip current!" Moe thought to himself.

Then, at the top of his lungs, he yelled, *"I am caught in a rip current!"*

Moe asked himself, *"What do I do? What did my dad say?"* He heard his dad's voice like he was sitting next to him on his board, *"Moe, the first thing you have to do is relax! Then, focus on the solution."*

Panicking clouds your judgement and wastes energy.
Relax and focus on the solution.

So, Moe took a deep breath and allowed the current to carry him. He stopped paddling against the current and just floated calmly. He finally realized that if he fought the current, he would tire himself out and he would be left without energy to paddle.

Moe began to relax, conserve his energy and to think about his situation. He thought: *"Now, let me see. Which way is this current taking me? Oh no, the current is taking me to those big jagged rocks. I am going to crash on those rocks, oh no! "*

The universal sign for trouble when you are in the ocean is waving your arms.
If you think you are in danger, attract the attention of nearby surfers or swimmers!
In foggy conditions, stay close to shore where you are visible.

Moe again remembered his dad's words, took a deep breath and relaxed allowing the current to carry him. But it continued to carry him towards the rocks. Moe was not happy about that, but he knew he could not fight the current. He continued to flow with the current. Slowly but steadily, he paddled parallel to the shoreline getting just a few inches closer to the beach.

Moe was drifting closer and closer to the rocks. At times he thought he was going to crash his board right on top of them. The edges of the huge boulders looked like razor-sharp fangs of some ancient sea monster. The half-submerged rocky formations got so close, he could almost touch them. Moe closed his eyes and said, *"Please, GOD, help me!"*

When he opened his eyes, the rocks were still alarmingly close, but he realized that he was no longer moving. He was sitting right in front of them, bobbing in the water, like a buoy at sea. The current had finally released him.

Moe started to paddle towards the beach. He felt elated. With just a few strokes, Moe was safe on the beach. Feeling sand in between his toes loosened the knot in his stomach. He finally was able to take a deep breath.

Rip currents always weaken at some point. Remember, go with the flow, then swim sideways, parallel to the beach. The most effective way to deal with rip currents is to **NEVER GO IN THE OCEAN ALONE**. Do your best to go to beaches with a strong swimmer or where there is a lifeguard.

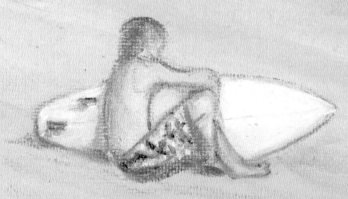

Moe was so thankful for the people in his life who had told him surf stories.

His Auntie Tia's story would always remind him to watch the surf before he went out. Moe's mom had taught him about paddling too far out, and uncle Kawika had taught him about the Stingray Shuffle.

But his dad's story had saved his life. It had given him the knowledge to be able to get out of the rip current safely.

From now on, Moe would pay close attention to his family and friends whenever they wanted to tell their surf stories.

You never know when your life will depend on them!

Info. Session

1. What do you think is the most important advice about avoiding trouble in the ocean?
2. What should you do if you are caught in a rip tide?
3. What did Moe learn from his Auntie Tia about the ocean?
4. Why is that important?
5. Why should you never go surfing alone?
6. What is the universal sign for being in danger when you are in the ocean?
7. What two major factors can prevent people from seeing you from shore?
8. If you are learning to surf, what kind of wave should you look for?
9. What are the different flags posted by US lifeguards?
10. Why should you be extremely careful when jumping off your surfboard?
11. What is the Sting Ray Shuffle?
12. If you find yourself in trouble, what are the two most important steps you should take?

1. Listen to your elders, especially your parents, lifeguards and those with more experience. Always treat the ocean with respect!
2. Swim or paddle with the current so that you will not get tired. Stay parallel to the beach and don't fight the current.
3. Always watch the ocean before going out. A rule of thumb is at least 10 minutes. When it is bigger, you may have to look at the ocean for a longer period.
4. You may show up at the beach while a lull is happening and you will not be able to see how big it is out there.
5. You should always have someone to rely upon in case you get in trouble. Use the BUDDY SYSTEM!
6. Waving your arms if you are in trouble will attract other people's attention. Remember, it is best to surf near a lifeguard.
7. Fog or night time. If fog starts to roll in, make sure to stay very close to shore. If dusk is approaching give yourself plenty of time to paddle in before night time arrives.
8. You should find a gentler breaking wave, which is not so steep and mostly just rolls in.
9. Green means safe to go; yellow means be careful; red means dangerous; yellow with a black ball means NO SURFING
10. Because it could be shallow or there could be a rock underneath the surface of the water.
11. Dragging your feet on the sand whenever walking out to the surf to avoid stepping on Sting Rays.
12. Relax and focus on the solution.

One Ocean. One Family.

Do you know where storm drains dump? They flow to our oceans. All trash that you see on streets or highways will drain to the ocean in time. Sometimes, it goes first into rivers and pollutes the land as waste makes its way into the ocean. Throwing garbage on the street is the same as throwing it into the ocean. Sea animals can mistake garbage for food and get sick from eating it!

We are all part of this planet. It takes all of us to help maintain our oceans. Here are 4 things that you can do to help keep our oceans healthy:

1. Recycle!
When you go to the beach, pack your own trash and a little of someone else's too. By making sure that the trash is placed in a garbage can and recycled, not only at the beach, but in our neighborhoods, we will help prevent sea animals from getting sick and their homes from being polluted. This way, we will still be able to enjoy riding waves with the dolphins!

2. Scoop the poop!
Pet waste can make both people and animals sick if it reaches the ocean. Always clean up after your pets in your yard, on the streets and sidewalks.

3. Think outside the box!
Make your own toys and make them so that they are friendly to our environment. Discover new ways of helping out our ocean. Learn about what causes harm to our beautiful beaches and what helps wildlife grow healthy again.

4. Lead by Example!
If you see someone throwing trash at the beach or on the street, pick their trash up and mentally thank them for giving you the opportunity to do the right thing.

Our oceans are all connected in the same way that the planet is all connected, and exactly how all human beings are connected. This is what **ONE OCEAN, ONE FAMILY** means to us. Let us take care of our playground together!

Ke'olu'olu e kokua e malama i ke kahakai.
(Please, always help to keep our oceans and beaches clean.)

THE END